RISE
Affirmations for Personal Growth

Book 3

By
Yesi Morillo

For My Sons
Branden Jesse & Nicholas Rey
who ride the storm with fun and laughter,
always infusing me with LIFE!

For My Queen
Prudencia Almanzar Bueno
who taught me to get up after every fall,
and who will continue to guide my path and look over me.
May You Rest in Peace, Mom.
March 1, 2020

and…

For The Greatest Warrior I've Ever Known
Natalia Harris
who taught me, and the world
how to be relentless, do the work,
and follow your dreams… against. all. odds.
May You Rest in Power, Nati.
May 6, 2020

We all need a little inspiration.
That small nudge to get us excited about ourselves,
and progressive with our future.

This gem of a book is your nudge.

It is here not just to inspire you,
but to remind you that you have
the power and courage
to create the life you truly desire.

It is all inside of you...
everything you need to make things happen.

Couple the elements of power and
courage with action,
and your greatness will be elevated
to effect change for yourself, and others.

Your greatness is exactly what
the world awaits – unleash it!

Be Your Own Ride or Die.

Who Are You Here To Be?

Get crystal clear on your desires,
dreams and goals
then COMMIT EVERYTHING
inside of you to make it all happen.

The best "revenge" is massive success.

Move forward, even when you're scared.
Move forward, *especially* when you're scared.

The only power people have over you,
is the power that you give them.

Stop watering dead plants…
When the seeds are poorly planted,
no amount of feed will revive them.
Let them go.
They will ruin your beautiful garden.

When you don't speak your mind,
or let things go you hold on to shit.

Shit brings you down, fogs your senses,
and cripples your mojo.

Shit attracts shit, slows your body down,
interrupts your sleep and
messes with your peace of mind

Point?

Speak your mind.
Let it go. Drop the shit.

Seek deep within.
Everything you need
is already inside of you.

Get your mind right.
Your most prized possession is
a mind of healthy, positive
and intentional thoughts.

Conviction, faith and grit.
The three ingredients of goal execution
self-elevation, and
the realization of your dreams.

Focus your mind and energy on the things
that are within your control.
All else, leave to the universe...
it *always* has your back.

Your power is not diminished by pain.
You are capable of progressing and thriving
even in your darkest moments.
Trust yourself. Trust the process.

Your test is your testimony.
Your trials and tribulations are the story
that will inspire others.

Share your story of overcoming confidently,
shamelessly and apologetically, then
watch the community around you flourish.

If you really want it, fight like hell for it.
Stop at nothing for your goals – commit to
them daily until you have accomplished
what you want.

Don't wait for something to happen
for YOU to happen.

YEARN.
Never stop wanting a higher level,
a happier environment, and the simplicity
of peace and joy.
All is possible.

Quit telling yourself ridiculous lies.
Don't even entertain negative thoughts that
go against the power, knowledge
and potential you possess.

A loss over something that served you no purpose is no loss at all - it is freedom, and freedom is delicious!

You are not your circumstances.
Your past is not your forever story
You have the power to write a new one.

Finish *unfinished* business.

Practice deep, deep gratitude.
Daily.

Your potential is much
bigger than your problem.
Take a step back. Take two.
Recalibrate.
Now get up,
and get back to living out
your true calling.

Design your own happy.
No one is responsible for
your beautiful joy but YOU.

You get light by walking through the dark.
Walk through the dark in your full power,
knowing that on the other side
is extraordinary success.

Be relentless in your endeavors.
Push through to achieve your dreams
against all odds – doing *whatever* it takes.

Not everyone deserves access.
Choose wisely who you share with, who you
engage with and who you spend your time
and energy on.

Your fire is always LIT!
Even in the toughest moments, your light
may dim, but it is never extinguished.
Trust that light.

Don't dim your light to
make others feel secure.
Shine Brighter. Buy 'em sunglasses.

There's nothing from the past to change,
only the present to heal
and the future to build.

You are a beautiful, imperfect BADASS!
Accept it!

Take your soul work serious.
The planting of passion in the depth of your
soul is of no coincidence.
Your responsibility is to execute that passion
with tenacity and purpose.

You have more power thank you think...
and you're doing much
better than you know.

Trust your intuition. It never lies.
Listen to your intuition.
It has all the answers.

Don't ever forget who you are!
A powerful being capable of anything!

You are limitless!

Face yourself.
Be truthful with yourself.
Covering up lies, and avoiding the hard
things only cripples your
ability to move forward.

You are a force to be reckoned with!
No one is as special, unique
and as tough as you!

Your purpose and passion is in your gift,
not in your title.

It is not how hard you fall,
it's how high you rise!
Fall hard… RISE high!

You can grow from broken.
We've all been derailed, experienced loss
and disappointment, but none of that
defines you.
Embrace the lesson, let go,
and get into relentless action.

You. Gotta. GRIND. To. GROW.

Replenish your soul with love,
laughter and fun.

When your soul is not nourished and
replenished, you will burn out.
Feed your soul... generously.

Life is an adventure filled with ups, downs
and deep disappointments.
You were designed for the ride.

Just because something has "always been"
doesn't mean it has to "always be".
Change is essential for growth.

If you asked for it, be ready to receive it.
The universe is ALWAYS listening
and it will deliver what you work for.
Get ready.

Conquer fear with courage and laughter...
the mix of perfect *progression medicine*
for the heart and soul.

Self-Love. Practice it. Often.
Love Yourself. Hard.

You are a brilliant, beautiful and bold.

Quit babysitting bullshit.
Enough of tolerating people
and things that do not serve you.

Never minimize your work,
skills or who you are to ease
someone else's insecurity.

Winning. Losing.
It's all the same.
The real goal is growth
and whether you're winning or losing,
you're constantly growing...
keep moving.

Set your intention.
Believe with everything you have
in your intention.
Live your intention...
stopping at nothing until
you get to where you need to be.

No one succeeds alone.
Create an entourage of
unbreakable support.
Create your tribe and love them hard.

Level up!
Choose who you associate with,
what you focus on,
and where your energy goes.
Choose wisely.

You are more than enough just the way you are, and you need zero validation to be exactly what you want to be.

YOU
are what you have been waiting for.

It is not the mind that decides.
It is the heart.
Listen to your heart,
for it knows your direction,
biggest desires and
what you are yearning for.

Then follow your heart…
it will lead you right down
your destined path.

What's on the back burner
that's been burning
a hole in your soul?
Start it. Now.

No more fuckery…
BOSS UP!
This is *your* time to dream big,
execute big, and succeed in a big way.
Let's go!

Fear is a choice.
Choose to be FEAR _LESS_.

You are light, potential and progress.
You are possible.
Illuminate a path of possibilities.

When things don't work out
exactly how you planned,
don't dwell on disappointment.

Pick yourself up,
rework your plan and
keep pressing forward.

There's another way.
There is always another way.
Find the way.

Choose Forward. Always.
Forward momentum, against all odds,
with power and grace.

Speak IT into existence.
You know what you want – put it out into the universe.
Then put in the work and watch it all come together.

Real moves are made in silence.
Work diligently, intentionally and quickly –
without having to announce your every
move in hopes of approval.
Your heart knows what's working in your
favor, trust it.

Stop asking for permission,
acceptance and validation.
You don't need any of these to
launch a dream, move yourself forward
or be who you want to be.

Live everyday with
DEEP INTENTION.
Spend zero time entertaining what does not
contribute to your well-being and growth.

Whatever hurts the most is the most
beneficial to you.
Learn. Adapt. Excel.
~ Branden Jesse
(my son)

We have moments in life where we mess up
so bad, it feels like there's no way out.
But trust that once you're at the bottom,
the only way out is up.
~ Nicholas Rey
(my son)

Pay it forward.
Your greatest gift is
the one you give away.

Keep Rising!

If you loved this book,
buy one for someone you love,
or for someone you believe
needs to be uplifted.

Also check out
RISE: THE JOURNAL

Purchase This Gem At
yesimorillo.com

About The Author
Yesi Morillo

Yesi Morillo is a former Wall Street executive
and award-winning entrepreneur.

Prior to her current role in government,
Yesi held a senior executive role in financial services.
She leads a for-profit leadership development
organization for women, Proud To Be Latina,
all while completing her Ph.D.
and raising two teenage sons.

A TEDx speaker, author and empowerment expert,
Yesi works to empower others to rise up to their full potential.

Connect with Yesi at
YESIMORILLO.COM
or on social media

YESIMORILLO
AND
PTBLATINA

YESIMORILLO
AND
PTBLATINA

RISE
Affirmations for Personal Growth
Book 3
Yesi Morillo

Other Titles By Yesi Morillo
RISE: Book 1
RISE: Book 2
RISE: The Journal
and
STAY – A Novel

Purchase all at yesimorillo.com

Made in the USA
Middletown, DE
19 June 2022